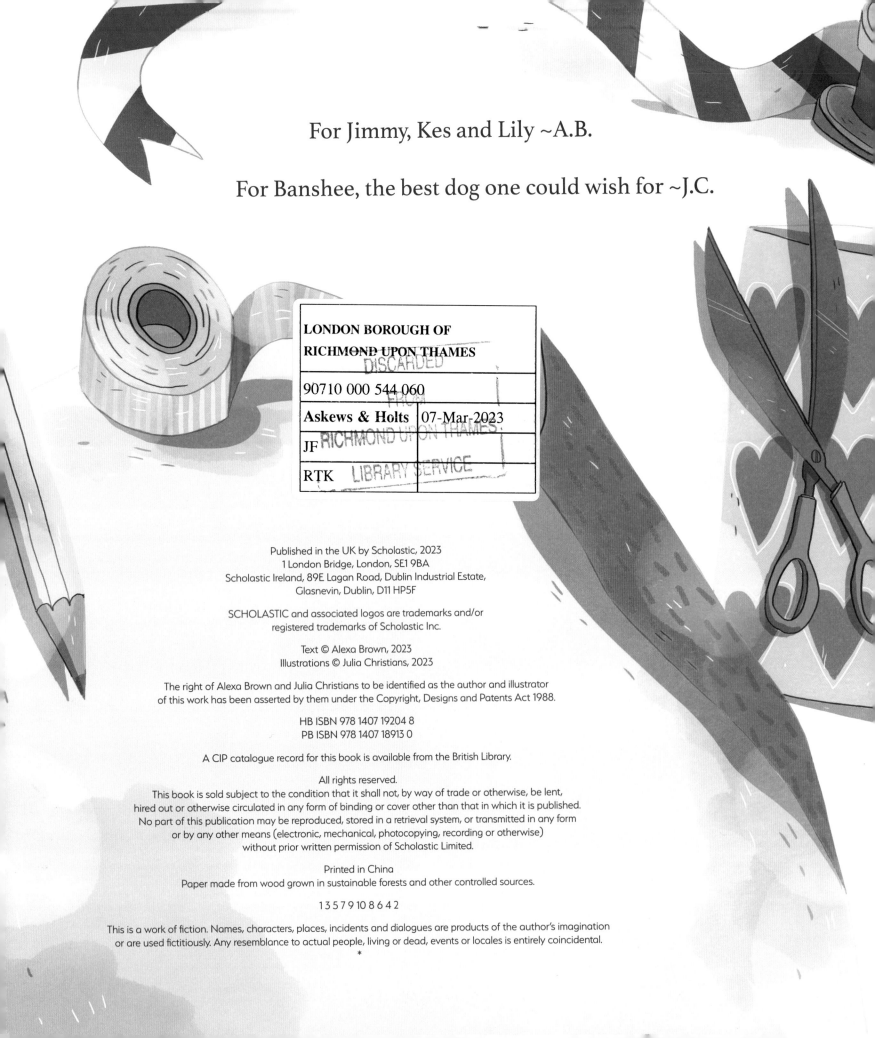

For Jimmy, Kes and Lily ~A.B.

For Banshee, the best dog one could wish for ~J.C.

Published in the UK by Scholastic, 2023
1 London Bridge, London, SE1 9BA
Scholastic Ireland, 89E Lagan Road, Dublin Industrial Estate,
Glasnevin, Dublin, D11 HP5F

SCHOLASTIC and associated logos are trademarks and/or
registered trademarks of Scholastic Inc.

Text © Alexa Brown, 2023
Illustrations © Julia Christians, 2023

The right of Alexa Brown and Julia Christians to be identified as the author and illustrator
of this work has been asserted by them under the Copyright, Designs and Patents Act 1988.

HB ISBN 978 1407 19204 8
PB ISBN 978 1407 18913 0

A CIP catalogue record for this book is available from the British Library.

Printed in China
Paper made from wood grown in sustainable forests and other controlled sources.

1 3 5 7 9 10 8 6 4 2

*

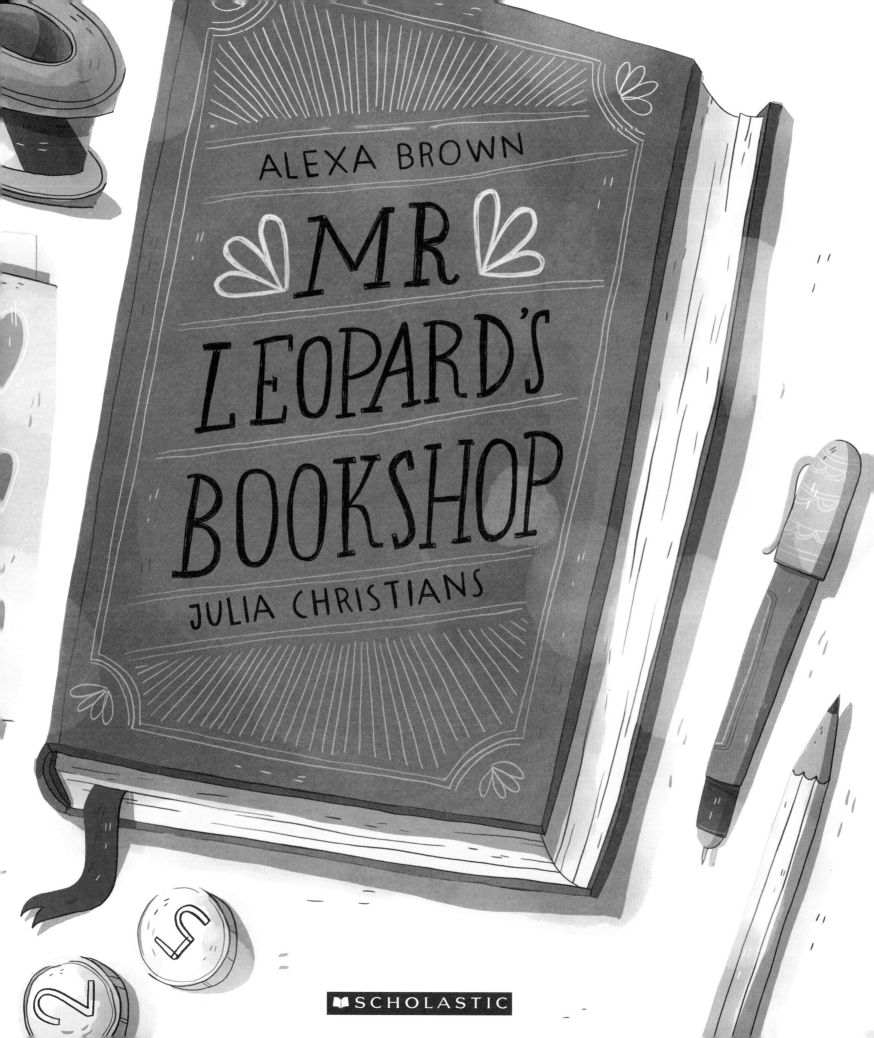

Sophie's best friend was her curly-tailed pug.
She loved his wet **kisses** and wriggly **hugs**.

His fur was like velvet, his nose black and shiny.
Boss was his name. He was ever so tiny.

Sophie was shopping today with her mum.
She needed a gift for her very best chum.
His birthday was soon and she'd started to worry.

"The shops are all shutting, Mum!
We need to hurry!"

But then Sophie noticed a shop up the road.
Over the doorway, a lamp softly glowed.
The window was lit with a welcoming twinkle,
she pushed on the door and a bell gave a tinkle.

The bookshop was like **nothing** Sophie had seen –
the place was **magnificent** (but needed a clean).

Books bulged out of sacks and were stuffed on the racks,
they swayed in tall, tumbling dangerous stacks.

There was **SO** much to see in this **magical place** –
could Sophie be dreaming? (She blinked, just in case.)
For there, looking up from some papers he'd dropped . . .

Was the great
Mr Leopard
who managed the shop!

Sophie's mum *swooned*
and fell
down
in a
fright.

Mr Leopard laughed gently,
"There, there, I don't bite."

He bowed very deeply
and beckoned her near,
"If you're after a book,
then I'll help you, my dear!"

With a gulp, she explained. "It's a **present** I need,
and it's got to be really **quite special** indeed!"

He **leapt** on a counter – "**Come on, take a look!**" –
and **dived** through the **wobbling** towers of books.

Then he was off,
piling books in each paw,

making **mess** after **mess**
as he **crashed** through the store.

He picked out some good ones,
then great ones, and yet –

"No . . .

No . . .

And **no . . .**" (Sophie felt quite upset.)

"Boss is my **best friend** –
the **best** that there is –
I **must** find a present
with **sparkle** and **fizz!**"

He gave her a wink.
**"I can help,
I'm quite certain."**

And *slowly* he drew back
a velvety curtain . . .

Mr Leopard was beaming. "Forget **human** tales!
Our writers are **zebras** and **lions** and **snails!**
Our artists are **penguins** and **parrots**, you see…"
Mr Leopard was literally trembling with glee.

Sophie stood blinking and shaking her head – perhaps she had actually fainted instead?

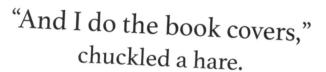

"I'm a historian," murmured a bear.

"And I do the book covers," chuckled a hare.

"Ghost stories? Sure!" the wolf gave a wink.

A squid raised a tentacle, "I make the ink!"

And then Sophie noticed
a dog on a rug,
with a pen in his paw . . .

It was **Boss**, her own pug!

"My goodness!" said Sophie. "This cannot be true!
There are animal authors, and **Boss** is one too?"

The creatures all bellowed a **deafening** cheer,
and Sophie hugged **Boss** as he nuzzled her ear.

"Now Boss,
it's **your** birthday,
so pick out a book."
The pup made his choice
after only one look:

*Baking a Cake Using
Dog Food, for Dummies.*

The dogs all applauded
and shouted out,
"Yummy!"

The bookseller smiled as he smoothed down his tail.
"I'll wrap that up now for you," warbled a whale.
They woke Sophie's mum, still passed out on the floor.
And then, with a wave, they went back through the door.

The very next day, Sophie put up balloons.
She lined up the knives and the forks and the spoons.

And, well, Boss's party went off with a **bang** –

Mr Leopard
turned up . . .

And he brought the whole gang!